Me-Shell The Mermaid Daughter

Sandi White

Illustrated by Nyda Bailey

To order additional copies of this book, contact:
Xlibris
1-888-795-4274
www.Xlibris.com
Orders@Xlibris.com

ISBN: Softcover   978-1-7960-9082-6
         Hardcover   978-1-7960-9083-3
         EBook   978-1-7960-9081-9

Library of Congress Control Number: 2020904125

Print information available on the last page

Rev. date: 03/27/2020

Acknowledgement

To my children, Lovebug#1 Myron, Lovebug#2 Nyda, Lovebug#3 Marlon II, and Lovebug#5 Malakhai, I thank you all for helping me keep the memory of your sister alive; my Lovebug#4 Me-Shell. May she continue to rest in peace. You are all my heart.

To my grandchildren, G-baby#1 Sa'Myra, G-baby#2 Celeste, G-baby#3 Maleigha, G-baby#4 Achilles, G-baby#5 London, and G-baby #6, I adore you all. A special note to my G-baby Zyara and her sister G-baby Madison, I love you. You were all my inspiration for this book.

A tremendous thanks to you my daughter Mrs. Nyda Bailey, for your hard work illustrating the book. I couldn't have done it without you. I love you. You did it while caring for and giving full attention to your daughters, 2-year-old London and 10-month-old Paris. Even with my help they were attached to you like little koala bears. To dress them, get them into the car seats, or the stroller, while Paris cried nonstop at times, to go pick up your 9-year old daughter Celeste from school, either driving or walking, is amazing. Walking in rain, snow, and cold weather with two small children is not easy. Keeping doctor appointments, cleaning up behind small children and supporting your husband are also difficult. I do appreciate your dedication illustrating the book.

To my Lovebug#5, Malakhai Browne, who was first tasked with illustrating this project, thank you for your effort. I know you could've done a great job but with school and the deadline to complete the book it was a little too much. We will do the next one together. I am especially proud of you for taking such good care of yourself since I have to work so much.

To my sisters, Lauretta White, Denisteen White, Leah Hobson, and Brenda Hobson, thank you for your encouragement and support through the years. We will never forget our brother Ephraim Hobson. May he continue to rest in peace. I love you all.

Extra special thanks to you, my cousins.

Rajendra Greenaway, you have always checked up on me to make sure that I was happy and well, even when you yourself were in worse situations than I were. I love you so very much. Michikoe Browne, you have given me the best birthday parties ever! I will cherish my memories with you until the end of time. Love you back!

To all my sisters, brothers, nieces and nephews, thank you all for always remembering me. You are in my heart and I deeply admire each of you individually.

Special thanks to my best friends for your unending support through the years.

Jennifer Brown, you have always kept me on the path of never letting my guard down and keeping my head high.

Sherene Guyton (the pastor's wife, lol), you have kept me on the path to church and fun times with our church sisters. We all adore the tea parties at church.

Caryl Turner-Slay, you have kept me on the path to further education. I especially enjoy our wonderful and exciting getaway me times at the Golden Nugget in Atlantic City.

Sharon Chesney, you have always kept me up to date with life unexpected surprises and can always give me a good laugh.

To my friend Ellondia Smith, thank you for your support with the book. You were just as excited as I was when the illustrations were produced. You had a lot more patience than I did and kept me from going insane with anxiety to get the book on the market.

Last but not least, my gratitude to Xlibis' staff for your precedential customer service. All of you my assigned representatives were equally friendly, understanding and knowledgeable as always. You all worked together efficiently and professionally to get my books published, now and in the past. Thanks, I am grateful for your encouragement to become a published author and your dedication toward the production of my books.

Dedication

This book is in memory of my second Daughter Me-Shell J'Nya-Raven Browne (9/10/04-9/10/04, R.I.P.); my Dad William Benjamin White (R.I.P); my Brother Ephraim Mickey Orlando Hobson (R.I.P.); my two childhood best friends - sisters Naomi and Judith Eudovique (both R.I.P.).

The book is dedicated to my six Grand-children, Sa'Myra Allen, Celeste Sewall, Maleigha Allen, Achilles Allen, London Rose Bailey, and Paris Bailey; Zyara Bailey and Madison Bailey. My sons Marlon Browne, II and Malakhai Browne.

About Montserrat

- Tropical, West Indies, Lesser Antilles, territory of United Kingdom

- Nicknamed the "Emerald Isle of the Caribbean" by Irish settlers from the island of St. Kitts and the state of Virginia

- Nine beaches: Eight black sand, one white sand; Little Bay Beach has black sand

- Cuisine: Goat water - stewed goat meat

- 40 square miles (104 sq. km); 11 miles (18 km) long, 7 miles (11 km) wide; Pear Shaped

- Population: 1955 - 14, 233; 1960 – 11, 957; 1990 -10,615; 1995 – 9,848/decreased-relocation after the volcano erupted; 2000 - 4,929; 2011 – 4922; 2020 - 4,992.

- Self-governing Commonwealth territory/Governor

- Education: Free and mandatory – 5yrs-16yrs; Very little illiteracy; 2004 Montserrat community College; Other higher education location: University of the West Indies.

- 1977-1989 Music-Recording studio by George Martin the Beatles Producer; used by Paul McCartney, Rolling Stones, & Elton John, (damaged by Hurricane Hugo 1989) rebuilt in 2006 as Montserrat Cultural Centre – multiuse performing arts centre

- Radio: ZJB Radio Montserrat; Cable and satellite available

- Newspaper: Montserrat Reporter, published weekly; online edition more current

- People of origin: Carib Indians, Irish, African, British, North American, European, French

- Slavery: Started 1660's; Population: 1678 – 1,000; 1810 – 7,000 (outnumbered whites); Abolished 1834 – cost of sugar fell internationally..0

- Devastating Hurricanes/earthquakes – Between 1890 & 1936. Hugo, 1989

- Plymouth, the old capital was destroyed in 1997 by one of the Soufriere hills volcanic eruptions. The new capital is now located in Brades.

- Airport: 1997 W.H. Bramble Airport closed due to volcano; 2005 John A. Osborne Airport opened; Linked to other international airports by helicopter and ferry.

- Plantations – tobacco, indigo, cotton and sugar; Twentieth century major export– Sea island cotton. Tourism and agriculture were flourishing before the eruptions. Now depend on the UK and Canada. Currency – Eastern Caribbean dollar.

- In the 1990's Chances Peak, in the Soufriere Hills, was the highest on the island, 3,000 feet high, until its first eruption in history in July of 1995.

(Britannica.com)

This is a story of a family living in a village called Little Bay, on a pear-shaped island named Montserrat. The island is located in the Caribbean Sea. Montserrat is nicknamed the Emerald Isle of the Caribbean and boasts beautiful beaches of gray, black, and white sand as well as lush vegetation.

Long ago, here lived a couple on the island of Montserrat named Wayne and Naomi White. They wanted a baby but was unable to have children. They loved each other very much and often prayed that one day they will be blessed with at least one child. Naomi loved walking on the black sandy beach of her village, gathering shells. She took the shells home and used them to decorate plaques.

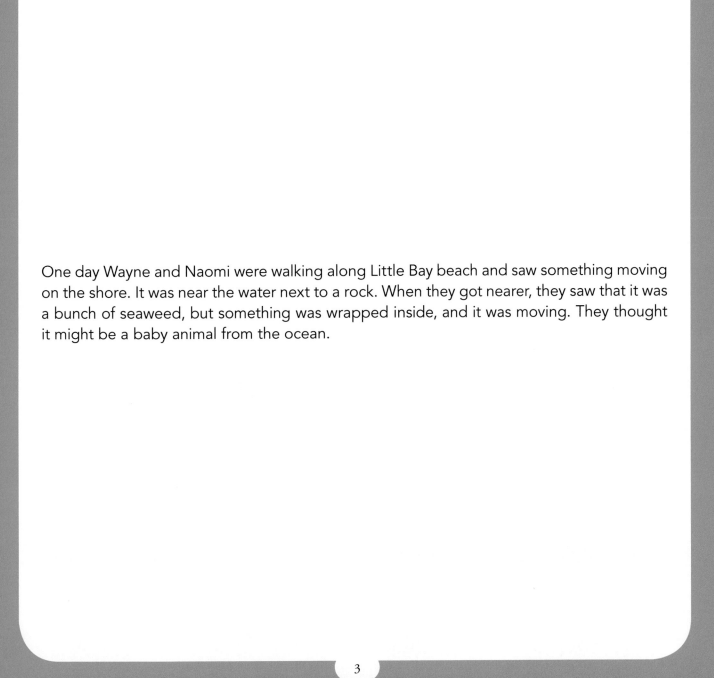

One day Wayne and Naomi were walking along Little Bay beach and saw something moving on the shore. It was near the water next to a rock. When they got nearer, they saw that it was a bunch of seaweed, but something was wrapped inside, and it was moving. They thought it might be a baby animal from the ocean.

They knelt, and when they opened the seaweed, they were surprised to see a beautiful baby with golden brown hair inside. They looked out at the ocean to see if any wreckage were floating around as to where the baby might have come from. All they saw was a dolphin swimming back and forth near the reef. They picked up the baby; it laughed and reached up to them. The couple looked up and said, "Thank you, God, for answering our prayers." They were very happy. The seaweed was wet, and the baby wasn't wearing any clothes. Naomi picked up the baby and cuddled it in her arms to keep it warm, although it was a hot day. Then she and Wayne started home with the baby still wrapped in the seaweed. They lived nearby, so they didn't have far to travel. As they walked away, they looked back at the ocean, but the dolphin was gone.

When Wayne and Naomi got home and unwrapped the baby from the seaweed, they were shocked to find that the baby had no legs but had a fin tail like a fish. A baby mermaid? Is there such a thing? Well, they had to believe. It was right in front of their eyes. One thing was for sure, they couldn't tell if it was a boy or a girl. Anyway, they dried the baby and wrapped it in blankets.

They wanted to feed the baby, but what do baby mermaids eat? They had no clue. So they decided to give the baby some milk. They fed the baby, had their dinner, and all went to bed. Before they fell asleep, they decided that they would go back to the beach the next day to try and figure out how the baby mermaid ended up on the beach and if the parents were looking for it. They also decided that if they found nothing after one week, they would keep the baby, name it, and raise it as their own.

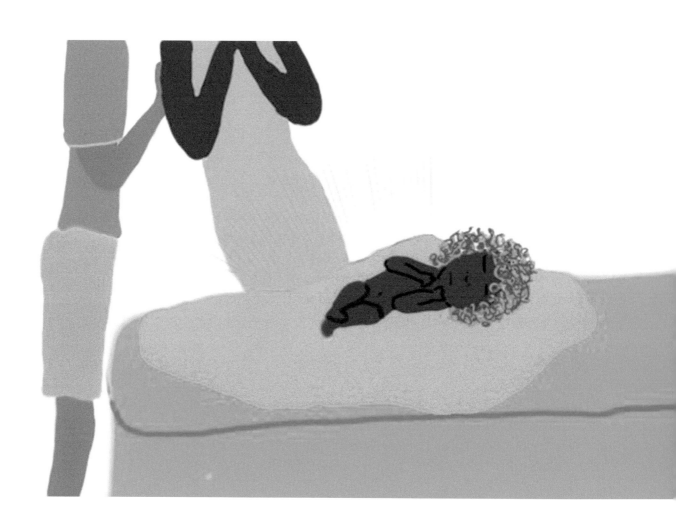

When they woke up the next morning, they were even more shocked to find out that the baby had legs, and it was a girl. They both believed it was a sign that the baby was sent for them. Naomi said, "What a miracle!" She made a diaper for the baby. However, they kept their promise to go back to the beach for one week and search for any sign of the baby mermaid's family. They did not find or see anything, so Naomi named the baby Me-Shell. She did so because she loved gathering shells from the beach, and since they found the baby on the beach, it was her special and most beautiful shell. They took Me-Shell to the beach daily. She loved the water. Wayne taught her to swim. He and Naomi weren't surprised that Me-Shell was a fast learner and a very good swimmer at such a young age.

Me-Shell grew up a very happy child. She was very intelligent, kindhearted, obedient, beautiful, and brave. She helped all her friends at school. She adored swimming and loved taking bubble baths. As Me-Shell grew older, she spent all her spare time at the beach as if the water called her. She was very competitive and a great swimmer, won every race that involved swimming, and could stay under water longer than anyone else. She also loved the underwater view of the ocean. Me-Shell was good at running. She loved racing with the boys because she'd always beat the girls.

She had two best friends, Zyara and Malakhai. They were both thirteen years old. Zyara had a seven-year-old little sister named Madison. Madison followed her almost everywhere she went. Malakhai had an elder brother named Marlon II. He was twenty years old. He worked almost every day, so they spent time together when possible. Me-Shell and Malakhai would often race on their way home after school. She could beat all the boys at running, but she could never beat Malakhai. Zyara and Madison would clap and cheer when they raced; they always hoped Me-Shell would win. After doing her homework and house chores, Me-Shell would go to the beach and swim for hours. She never seemed to get enough of swimming in the big blue sea.

There was one thing Me-Shell did not understand. For as long as she could remember, her parents would not allow her to go swimming on her birthdays. She was only allowed to take bubble baths as long as she would like. The other children got to go to the beach on their birthdays. *Why not me?* she thought. After all, why couldn't she go to the beach on her birthday to do the one thing she loved the most, swimming? On the day after her birthdays, she would ask her friends "How was the beach?" and if they went swimming. They'd always answer, "It was no fun without you" and "Yes, we did go swimming. The water was warm!" But last year, after her fifteenth birthday, their answers were "The waves were a little too high, so we didn't go swimming. We just wet our feet in the waves as they rolled onto the sand," "The water felt like it was grabbing our legs, but then it would let go," "Weird," and "However, still no fun without you." Me-Shell knew that her parents found her on the beach when she was three months old. What Me-Shell did not know was that she had a mermaid fin tail as a baby when Wayne and Naomi found her on the beach. What else didn't she know?

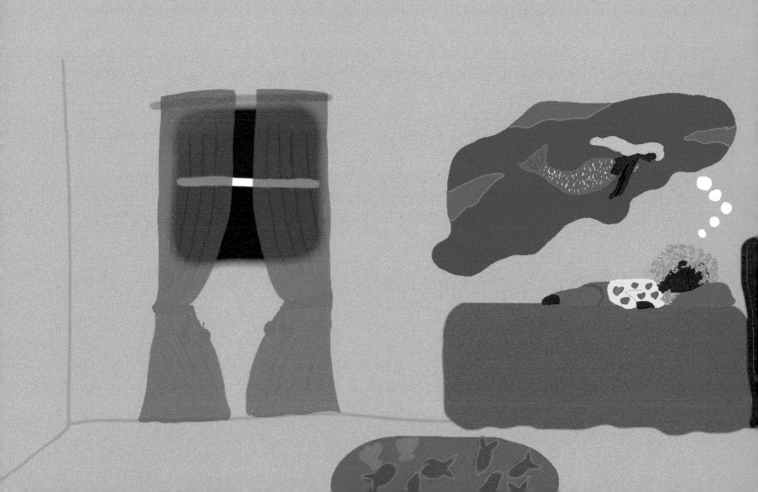

As Me-Shell grew older, she often dreamed of being a mermaid swimming deep under the ocean. It was very beautiful every time, and she was never afraid. Although she was always by herself, she felt like she was not alone. However, this year, prior to her sixteenth birthday, the dreams became more frequent and vivid. In them, she felt as though someone was watching her and calling her by a familiar name, but she did not recognize it. She could never remember the name when she woke up.

Whenever she told her mother about her dreams, her mother would smile and say, "Well, maybe you are a mermaid, my daughter. After all, your father and I found you on the beach." She would kiss Me-Shell on her forehead and say, "Now run along and go play with your friends." Me-Shell would smile and say, "I love you, Mommy." And Naomi would reply, "I love you too, my mermaid daughter." They always laughed.

It always felt comfortable in the ocean when she was swimming as if she was born to swim. The ocean felt familiar to her, like it was home. She read books about mermaids and heard stories about them frequently, but the stories were always referred to as folklore. She started a collection of pictures and books about mermaids; she felt drawn to them.

All week long at school, her friends were curious if she would be able to go swimming on her birthday the coming weekend. Her friend Malakhai said to her, "Maybe when you go swimming on Saturday, you'll turn into a mermaid for your birthday." Everyone laughed. Me-Shell smiled at the thought. Her friends knew that she believed mermaids were real, and she loved talking about them, but only her best friends Zyara and Malakhai knew about her dreams.

It was Saturday, and finally, it was Me-Shell's sixteenth birthday. She was very excited because she was sure, that now she was older, her parents would allow her to go to the beach with her friends for her birthday. Me-Shell woke up bright and early before her parents, cooked breakfast, did all her chores, and waited to ask them to go swimming.

When her mother woke up and smelled the food, she said, "My daughter, it is your birthday. We are supposed to cook breakfast for you. By the way, what are your plans for a party today?"

Before she could answer, her father walked into the kitchen and said, "Well, what do we have here? The birthday girl cooked breakfast?" He leaned over and kissed Me-Shell on the forehead and said, "Happy birthday, my daughter."

Me-Shell smiled and said, "Thank you, Daddy." He then told her he would fix her a bubble bath, to which she replied, "I already took a bubble bath."

They both looked surprised. They looked at each other and then at her. Me-Shell then asked them if she could have her birthday party at the beach with her friends this year. It was the weekend, so she could spend the whole day swimming in the ocean. That was why she got up early and did all her chores and cooked them breakfast. Her parents looked at her sadly and then at each other.

Her father said, "Sorry, you can't . . .," and turned away. He was heartbroken that he could not grant his daughter her heart's desire.

Her mother said, "It is only because we care. We do it to protect you. Trust me, one day you will understand. We do love you, my daughter." Me-Shell started to cry.

Although she had never questioned her parents' decision before, she asked if something bad had happened to her on her birthday when she was younger. She explained that she was older now, they should not worry, and she will be okay. But her parents knew what would happen, and they would not give her permission to go swimming. This was the first sad birthday for Me-Shell and the first time that she and her parents had a disagreement. She knew that her friends were all expecting to see her at the beach today for her birthday party, especially Zyara and Malakhai. She went to her room, lay on her bed, and cried.

Me-Shell was determined that she was going swimming on her birthday. She got up and got dressed in a short blue blouse and pink short pants. She told her mother she was going into town to shop for her party dress. She went into town with Zyara. Me-Shell told her that after buying her dress, she was going swimming. Zyara said, "What about your parents?" Me-Shell said, "I will tell them when I get back home. They will see I will be all right." After picking out a very beautiful dress, they both headed for the beach. Malakhai, Madison, and their other friends joined them along the way.

When they arrived, they were all surprised to see that the waves were the same as the year before, a little too high for swimming. Zyara said to Me-Shell, "This is exactly what happened last year on your birthday." Me-Shell said, "I'm not afraid. I'm going swimming." She took off her pink shorts, and wearing her bikini bottoms and blue blouse, she started walking toward the water. Her friends started yelling at her to get back. The minute the water touched her feet, it swirled up around her legs and seemed to pull them toward the ocean. Me-Shell could not resist the urge to go swimming. For some unknown reason, she was not afraid. She actually thought she heard someone calling her by the name in her dreams. She knew it was her name; it was familiar but unfamiliar. She still could not make out what the voice was saying. Also, it seemed as though she was the only one who could hear the voice calling her. She was hypnotized.

As she moved forward into the water, her two best friends went into the water and tried to pull her back, but they could not move her backward; she just kept moving forward. The water had ahold of Me-Shell's legs while the waves pushed her friends out of the water. They had never felt such force from the waves before. The water was up around Me-Shell's knees now, and it moved her further into the ocean. When Me-Shell got in up to her waist, she suddenly disappeared under the surface. Her friends were terrified. They started crying and calling out her name. But Me-Shell was nowhere to be seen. After Me-Shell disappeared under the water, the ocean became very calm, so calm it was as if the water stopped moving. It seemed to have gotten what it was searching for, so it became quiet. Malakhai and some of the children ran to get Wayne and Naomi. Zyara, Madison, and others stayed at the beach and kept calling for Me-Shell. They were afraid to go back into the ocean for fear they would disappear under the ocean too.

Malakhai and the other children arrived at Me-Shell's house running, yelling, and screaming for help. Wayne and Naomi ran out in confusion, trying to understand what the commotion was about. When they understood what Malakhai was saying, they both ran as fast as they could to the beach. Naomi was crying. Wayne ran into the water. He dove and swam as far as he could go, calling and searching for Me-Shell. He could not find her. He got out of the water crying and went to console Naomi.

Some of the people from the village came to the beach to help search for Me-Shell. Malakhai, Zyara, and the other children were crying because they were scared and believed that Me-Shell drowned. They felt responsible for encouraging her to go to the beach for her birthday. Wayne and Naomi were crying because they believed that Me-Shell was lost, afraid, and alone, not knowing why she had a fin tail and was able to breathe under water. They were most afraid that she would get hurt by sharks or other predators in the ocean. She wouldn't know how to protect or defend herself. Wayne and Naomi kept faith that Me-Shell would survive and that her ocean family would find her. The women consoled Naomi, and the men consoled Wayne. The children all hugged one another and cried. The parents stayed with Wayne and Naomi until nightfall and then took their children home to bed. Wayne and Naomi stayed at the beach all night, hoping that Me-Shell would come back home like that time when she was two, but she didn't. They went home the next morning. Naomi was still crying her eyes out.

Each day they went back to the beach to wait for Me-Shell, and each day they left crying on the way home. This went on for months. Finally, things went back to normal. Believing that Me-Shell was gone for good, her parents prayed that she was with her ocean family. But they were still worried and blamed themselves for not telling her the truth earlier, that she was a mermaid.

It was one year later, and it was Me-Shell's seventeenth birthday. Malakhai, Zyara, Madison, and other friends of Me-Shell went to the beach that morning to honor her. The water was very calm. Wayne and Naomi were at the beach in hopes of seeing Me-Shell since it was her birthday. "Maybe she will come to visit us," Naomi said to Wayne. He smiled at her and nodded yes. They were there all morning. Other parents and friends stopped by to support Wayne and Naomi. People sat around on the beach looking out at the ocean for a while and then left as others came and went. Marlon stopped by too before going to work. Since Wayne and Naomi knew that Me-Shell was a mermaid, they were convinced that she was with her real parents and believed that she would return to visit them one day, maybe today because it was her birthday. Everyone else thought that Me-Shell drowned when she was pulled under the ocean by the waves on her birthday a year ago. Me-Shell's parents did not leave the beach until lunchtime.

Wayne and Naomi started walking away from the beach with Malakhai, Zyara, Madison, and some other children when they heard a voice say, "Mommy! Daddy!" They all turned around quickly and saw Me-Shell in the ocean waist-deep. Her friends thought, surely it must be a ghost. They were frightened. Then they noticed that all around her were other people—men, women, children, and babies. There were also dolphins swimming behind them. Everyone was surprised to see Me-Shell alive, although Wayne and Naomi were surprised for another reason, the fact that Me-Shell came back to see them. However, they were all surprised to see other "people" with her in the ocean and so many of them. Before she could think twice, Naomi ran toward the ocean and into the water. She hugged Me-Shell tightly and cried. They were both happy to see each other. Me-Shell hugged her and Wayne, who had joined them. They had so many questions for Me-Shell, so did her friends and everyone else who came running to the beach after they heard the news. They had to see it to believe it. Me-Shell could not walk out of the water because she had no legs, but the only people on land who knew that were Wayne and Naomi.

Wayne and Naomi came out of the water and faced their people to tell them a story, a story about Me-Shell. People were asking why Me-Shell stayed in the water. Naomi said she would explain. Everyone sat on the beach and listened. Everyone, including Me-Shell, knew that her parents found her on the beach when she was just three months old. What they did not know was that Me-Shell had a mermaid fin tail as a baby when Wayne and Naomi found her. Naomi told her story to them. Everyone in the ocean listened too. Naomi started with the day she and Wayne saw Me-Shell on the beach wrapped in seaweed right up until the day she disappeared. Everyone listened keenly. For two years on her birthday, her legs became fin-tailed when they took her swimming in the ocean. That was how the bubble bath tradition came about. That was also how they decided what date and month would be her birthday so they could keep track of her transformation date. She told Me-Shell and everyone else that was why they never allowed her to go into the ocean on her birthday. Malakhai laughed and said, "Last year, as a joke, I told her maybe she would turn into a mermaid if she goes swimming on her birthday." Well, that was exactly what happened.

This is how their story went. Wayne and Naomi took Me-Shell to the beach daily until one day, when they took her into the ocean, it took them by surprise that her legs became fin-tailed again. They were so afraid that the other people at the beach would notice what happened that they wrapped her up and quickly took her home. But Me-Shell wanted to swim, so she cried and cried. Neither Wayne nor Naomi could console her. Her fin tail kept flipping back and forth on the bed. They were afraid that her legs would not return. Finally, Naomi decided to put her in the bathtub full of water. Me-Shell stopped crying and started playing in the water, and her fin tail soon became legs again. This did not seem to bother Me-Shell at all. She just kept splashing the water around. So Naomi decided to add some bubbles to the water, and that made Me-Shell very happy. She squealed with joy. It was a sound her parents had never heard her make before.

The next day, they took Me-Shell to the beach again when no one was around. There was a small open cave nearby, so they went to it. When they put her in the water, her legs did not change. They let her swim around on her own. So they went back to their routine of taking her to the beach every day.

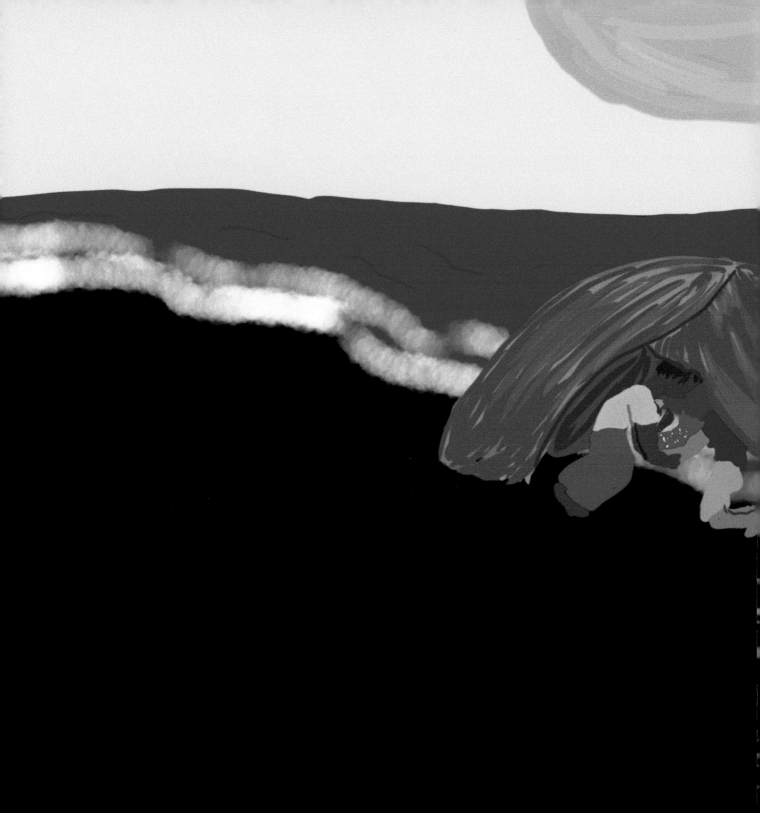

Another year went by, and it happened again; her legs became fin-tailed after they entered the ocean. They swam over to the open cave, out of view of other swimmers, and let Me-Shell swim to her heart's content. She was a great swimmer, very fast. At one point, she dove under the water and was under for so long they thought she was gone forever. Wayne and Naomi were so worried and feared that they would never see Me-Shell again. Naomi said, "Maybe her real parents found her and took her back." She was sad but happy for Me-Shell. Wayne hugged her. They decided to wait as long as it took to see if Me-Shell would return. They were happy when they saw her swimming toward them from far away in the ocean. When she entered the cave, she had shells and other beautiful stones she had found on the ocean floor. She kept saying, "Pretty fish." Again, they took her home all wrapped up and into the bathtub with bubbles. Me-Shell squealed with joy, that sound they never heard her make on a regular basis except when her legs changed to fin tail.

Wayne and Naomi decided to make that day Me-Shell's birthday. She was now two years old. The date will be recorded as the day her legs would disappear whenever she went into the ocean. Since her fin tail changed back to legs, they decided to have a birthday party and invited the other parents to bring their children over to celebrate with Me-Shell. That was when Me-Shell met Malakhai and Zyara. They became fast friends. However, Wayne and Naomi decided from that day forward they would not take Me-Shell to the beach on her birthday, nor would she be allowed to go to the beach on her birthday when she got older. It would become a tradition for her to take bubble baths at home on her birthday.

So on her third birthday, they kept her at home and prepared a bubble bath for her. Me-Shell had an amazing time laughing and playing in the bathtub full of bubbles. Although she did mention the beach a few times, she didn't make a fuss about it. The amazing thing was that her legs never changed to her fin tail. Henceforth, bubble bath tradition since then. Later that day, they had a birthday party for Me-Shell and invited her friends.

Everyone from the village was in awe when they learned that Me-Shell was a mermaid the whole time—with legs. Of course, they thought that she was human. After all, she had legs. They also found out that Me-Shell herself did not know she was a mermaid the entire time she lived in the village, not until the day she disappeared under the ocean. Now they understood why she adored swimming, won all the swimming races, and loved hearing and reading stories about mermaids.

When Naomi got to the day at hand, Me-Shell's seventeenth birthday, everyone on the beach looked out at the ocean as if for the first time they realized that people were in the water. Then all the mermaids, including Me-Shell, dove under the water, flipped their fin tails, and returned to the surface smiling. The people on the beach were all wide-eyed by the confirmation of Naomi's story about Me-Shell. They all started laughing because now they understood why Me-Shell stayed in the water after all.

Me-Shell then said to her family and friends on the beach, "Let me introduce you to my family and friends here with me." She gestured toward two mermaids who were wearing crowns (which no one had noticed until now) and said, "Meet my parents—my father, King William VI, and my mother, Queen Christeen III." She turned the other way and said, "Meet my sisters—Princesses Sa'Myra, Celeste, Maleigha, London, and Paris. Meet my brother, Prince Achilles, and my fiancé, Prince Ephraim IV. My fiancé met me on my sixteenth birthday and took me to my father's kingdom."

Me-Shell also told them that her original name was Princess J'Nya-Raven, the firstborn of the king and queen. Three months after birth, she was lost on a trip to Ephraim's kingdom. Everyone else were family and friends from their kingdom who came along for the trip. Malakhai and Zyara was jumping, laughing, and yelling, "Our best friend is a mermaid princess!" She told them her plan was to have her birthday party at the beach like she wanted to the year before. But this time it would be the best birthday party she would ever have because she got to celebrate with both her families and friends at the beach. She could swim and get out of the water and dance to her heart's content. She could go in and out of the water as much as she would like because it was her birthday. She turned and asked her mer-parents for permission to exit the water to go get ready for her birthday party. They both smiled, and her father said, "Yes. But if your fin tail starts tingling, that means it will transform into your legs."

Wayne went back into the water, picked up Me-Shell, and brought her onto the beach. Her fin tail glistened in the light. Naomi opened a white blanket onto the black sand. She always had it with her when she went to the beach in case Me-Shell showed up. She also had clothes for her. Wayne put Me-Shell to sit on the blanket, and her fin tail sparkled like a million jewels in the sunlight. She looked like a rare jewel on the black sand. Everyone on the beach, including her parents, thought it was one of the most beautiful things they had ever seen. They complimented her. Me-Shell smiled. She was the happiest she had ever been in her entire life.

Everyone gathered around. They all had so many questions, but all had to wait because her birthday celebration was at hand. However, she did tell them that she had a party for her sixteenth birthday with her mer-family at the kingdom and was very happy. But she was happier to celebrate this birthday with both her families and friends. She told them that her gift was rare among mermaids. So since her legs could only transform on her birthday, she could then decide where she wanted to live for the next year after, on land or in the ocean. Some other good news, her fiancé, Ephraim IV, was also born with the rare gift, one year before she did. Their parents agreed to allow them to get married when they grew up. They were supposed to grow up together, become friends, and then fall in love. But Me-Shell was lost as a baby.

She didn't know it then, but it was love at first sight when she and Ephraim first saw each other on her sixteenth birthday.

Me-Shell felt a tingling in her fin tail. She remembered what her mer-father told her before she left the water. She covered her fin tail with the blanket while it transformed into her legs. She then got up with the blanket wrapped around her and walked with Naomi to the cave to change into her clothes. She then waved to her mer-family and walked to the house with her mother to get dressed for her party. She took her traditional bubble bath and got dressed while Zyara waited for her. They went to town to shop for her dress. She bought a beautiful blue dress with silver sparkles on it. Malakhai and Madison went to the beach with others to decorate for the party. The party was held next to the small opened cave so that the mermaids could sit on the inside of it. The decorations were inside and outside the cave. Some of the villagers cooked food for the party. Everyone in the village attended. All businesses were closed for the rest of the day. The villagers swam with the mermaids.

Me-Shell was officially renamed by both sets of her parents Princess Me-Shell J'Nya-Raven. When she stayed with Naomi and Wayne, they would call her Me-Shell, and when she was with her family in the kingdom, they would call her Princess J'Nya-Raven. Me-Shell smiled and said, "Just call me Princess MJ." All agreed.

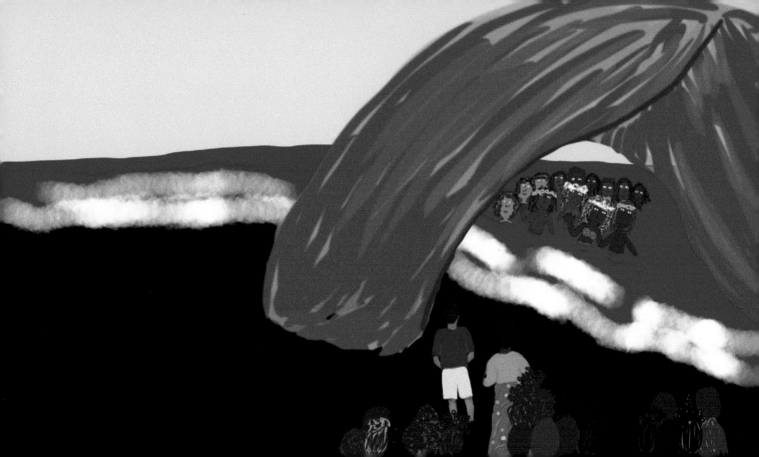

Everyone at the party ate, laughed, swam, danced, and told stories into the night. One story that was told by Princess MJ was about her engagement to Prince Ephraim IV. Tomorrow she would tell them about her year spent with her mer-family in the kingdom under the ocean. Zyara said, "I'm so happy for you, my best friend." They hugged each other. Me-Shell said, "Thank you, Zyara. I love you." Malakhai hugged her and said, "Proud of you, my best friend, and thanks for coming back to see us." Me-Shell laughed and said, "I love you both, so how could I live without my two best friends?" They all laughed and hugged each other again.

On the night of her seventeenth birthday party, it was agreed between both sets of parents that Princess Me-Shell J'Nya-Raven would spend the year with Wayne and Naomi, and the wedding would commence on her eighteenth birthday. The ceremony would be held on the island of Montserrat, on the beach of Little Bay. That way, everyone the princess loved on land and at sea would be able to attend. Prince Ephraim IV would visit her monthly until the wedding.

The months flew by quickly. All year, preparations were made for the wedding by both sets of the princess's parents. Everyone on the island was excited and could hardly wait for her wedding day.

Coming Soon
The Mermaid Daughter II
Princess Me-Shell J'Nya-Raven

Printed in the United States
By Bookmasters